Cosmo
THE DODO BIRD™

Cosmo is a dodo. He is one of a unique species of bird that once lived on our planet. Hundreds of years ago, he and the other [...] on the island of Mauritius, [...] and their charted land.

Approximately 300 years ago, and only a few years after the first sailors arrived on the island, the dodos had almost completely disappeared. Only Cosmo remained. He was the last dodo.

With his new friend, 3R-V the spaceship, Cosmo now travels from planet to planet in search of other dodos like him. Together Cosmo and 3R-V have great adventures.

Originally published as *Les Aventures de Cosmo le dodo de l'espace: La grande illusion* by Origo Publications, POB 4 Chambly, Quebec J3L 4B1, 2008

Copyright © 2009 by Racine et Associés
Concept created by Pat Rac
Editing and Illustrations: Pat Rac
Writing Team: Neijib Bentaieb, François Perras, Pat Rac

English translation © 2011 by Tundra Books
This English edition published in Canada by Tundra Books, 2011
75 Sherbourne Street, Toronto, Ontario M5A 2P9

Published in the United States by
Tundra Books of Northern New York
P.O. Box 1030, Plattsburgh, New York 12901

Library of Congress Control Number: 2010928801

Library and Archives Canada Cataloguing in Publication

Pat Rac, 1963-
[Grande illusion. English]
The great illusion / Patrice Racine.

(The adventures of Cosmo the dodo bird.)
Translation of: La grande illusion.
For ages 6-9.
ISBN 978-1-77049-248-6

I. Title. II. Title: Grande illusion. English.
III. Series: Pat Rac, 1963- .
Adventures of Cosmo the dodo bird.

PS8631.A8294G7413 2011   jC843'.6   C2010-903173-3

We acknowledge the financial support of the Government of Canada through the Book Publishing Industry Development Program (BPIDP) and that of the Government of Ontario through the Ontario Media Development Corporation's Ontario Book Initiative. We further acknowledge the support of the Canada Council for the Arts and the Ontario Arts Council for our publishing program.

ONTARIO ARTS COUNCIL
CONSEIL DES ARTS DE L'ONTARIO

For more information on the international rights, please visit www.cosmothedodobird.com

Printed in Mexico

1 2 3 4 5 6   16 15 14 13 12 11

MIX
Paper from responsible sources
FSC® C101537

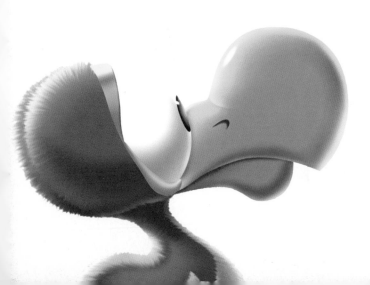

For all the children of the world

THE ADVENTURES OF
COSMO
THE DODO BIRD™

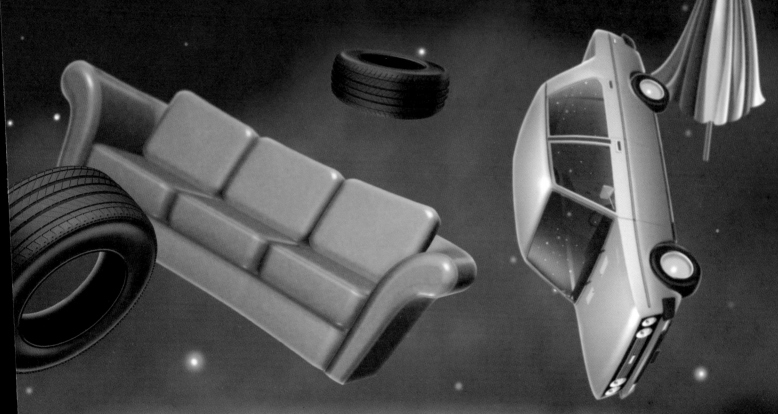

THE GREAT ILLUSION

Tundra Books

"Do you think we'll ever find other dodos like me, 3R-V?
 We've been traveling through space for ages."

"Don't be a discouraged dodo, Cosmo. Let's land at that planet. We're bound to find . . .
 Whoa! What in the universe!!!???"

Suddenly, Cosmo and 3R-V are dodging pop cans, an old car, and even used furniture.
They have to zigzag around a chest of drawers!

"Where is this stuff coming from?" cries Cosmo.

"Look over there! It's coming from that spot on the planet," says 3R-V.
"Let's go see!"

Curious, the two friends descend to the planet.

When 3R-V and Cosmo land, they are greeted by an odd little fellow in a tall, black hat.

Cosmo introduces himself politely. "Hello! I am Cosmo, and this is 3R-V.
We are searching for other dodos like me."

"And I am Zigor, the Great Illusionist. I am a magician."
Zigor points proudly to a poster with his picture on it.

"Are there dodos on your planet?" Cosmo asks hopefully.

"Perhaps." says the magician.

"If you do magic, could you make a dodo appear?"

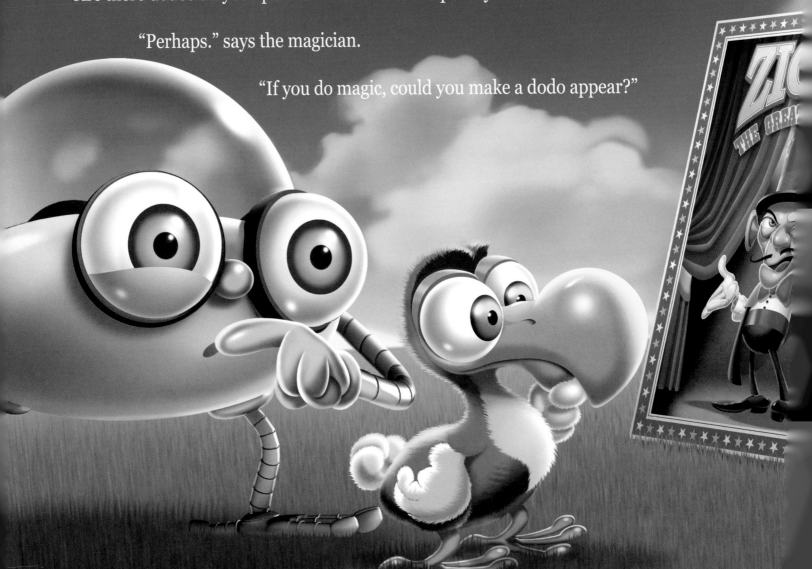

"Oh no, I make things disappear! It's far more useful!
The people of my planet bring me their rubbish.
And presto! I make that rubbish vanish.
Would you like a private performance?"

"Super!" says 3R-V.

From the stage, Zigor begins. "Ladies and gentlemen, girls and boys, prepare yourselves. You are about to witness a great magic trick!"

He pauses for a moment and waves his wand.

"I draw your attention to this old television behind me." Zigor taps it.

"In a few seconds, I will make it disappear."

Zigor raises his magic wand to the sky.

"Abracadabra, good riddance!"

No sooner has he cast his spell, than Zigor shouts, "Over there! Are those dodos?"

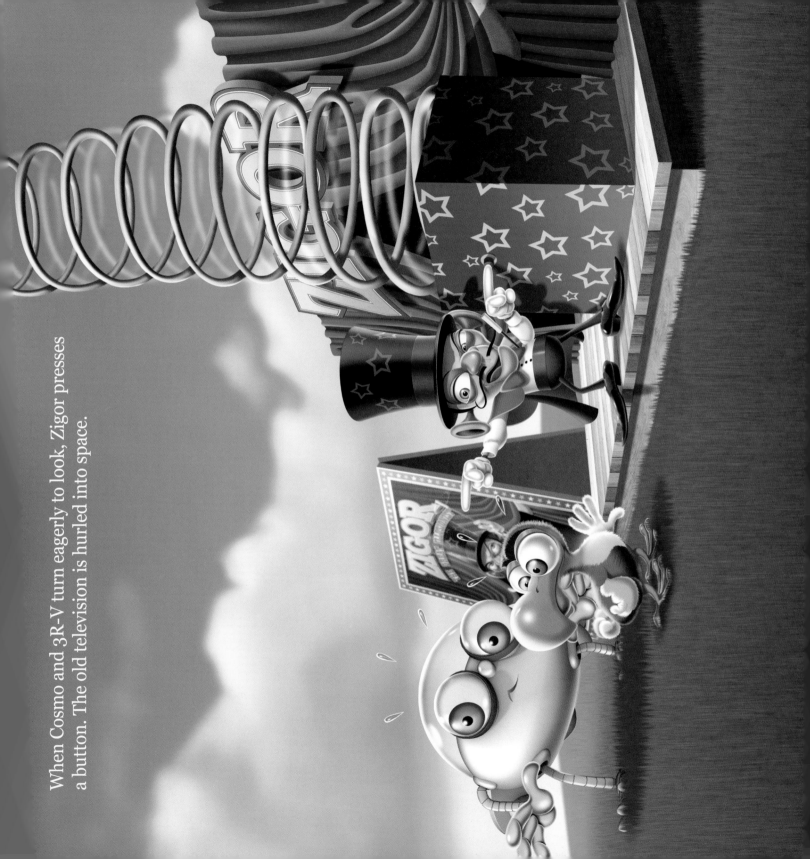

When Cosmo and 3R-V turn eagerly to look, Zigor presses a button. The old television is hurled into space.

Tadaaaam!

The television has disappeared!

Cosmo, almost in tears, turns back to Zigor. "There are no dodos here!"

"Perhaps not, but there is no useless television either!
You may now applaud," replies Zigor proudly.

Cosmo whispers to 3R-V, "Are you thinking what I'm thinking?"

"Yes! His trick is connected to all the junk we saw in space."

"Zigor, we know your trick!" shouts Cosmo. "You are making garbage disappear by sending it into space!"

Zigor puts a finger to his lips.

"*Sh!* Don't tell anyone.
All magicians have their secrets. . . ."

"You know, all the things you launched into space
will end up falling back down one day," says 3R-V.

"Zigor, all that junk might land on your head," adds Cosmo.

"Impossible! I am Zigor, The Great Illusionist.
I have done this magic act for a long time and nothing has ever fallen
from the sky!"

The words have just left his mouth, when a washing machine crashes to the ground. Zigor's stage shatters.

"Cosmo, look at the sky!" 3R-V is alarmed. A garbage storm is brewing!

The garbage rain is getting heavier and heavier. "Watch out!" 3R-V is so startled that he can't move.

"Quick! There's not a second to lose. Run for cover!" cries Cosmo.

As fast as it began, the garbage shower stops.

"What a disaster! All this garbage coming back and trashing your planet," moans Cosmo.

"What a disaster! All this garbage coming back and trashing my fame as a great illusionist," moans Zigor.

"Wait, where's 3R-V?"
Cosmo hasn't seen his friend since the garbage rain began. "I hope he's okay."

But 3R-V isn't okay. Cosmo finds him lying on the ground.

"Are you hurt?" cries Cosmo.

"My wing . . . it's broken. I won't be able to fly anymore. . . ."
3R-V's voice is weak.

"If I can't fly, we will never be able to continue our mission.
We will be stuck here forever. . . ." says 3R-V, before he faints.

Cosmo is angry. "See what your tricks have done, Zigor?
Now is the time for real magic!"

"Well, I *am* a real magician," mumbles Zigor, ashamed.

Suddenly, Zigor has an idea. He runs and grabs an old beach umbrella, then takes it over to 3R-V.

"I have more than one trick up my sleeve!"

Cosmo is suspicious. What is the magician planning?

"Come on, trust me," says Zigor.

Zigor opens the umbrella and hides himself and 3R-V.

"What are you doing? Leave my friend alone!" Cosmo is concerned.

"Don't worry! Everything will be all right!" Zigor finally begins: "Ladies and gentlemen, girls and boys, you are about to witness a grand magic trick – one that is larger than life. Abracadabra!"

Zigor lifts the umbrella.

Tadaaaam!

Cosmo is stunned. 3R-V is standing up and seems to be as good as new.

"My wing is perfect. Thank you very much, Zigor!"

"Wow! Zigor, you *are* a true magician!" adds Cosmo.

Zigor is proud of himself. "Did you like my new magic act?"

"It was fantastic!" cries Cosmo. "How did you do it?"

"All magicians have their secrets. But, I will tell you that I have learned that these old objects can be useful after all," replies Zigor.

"Now, that's real magic!" says Cosmo.

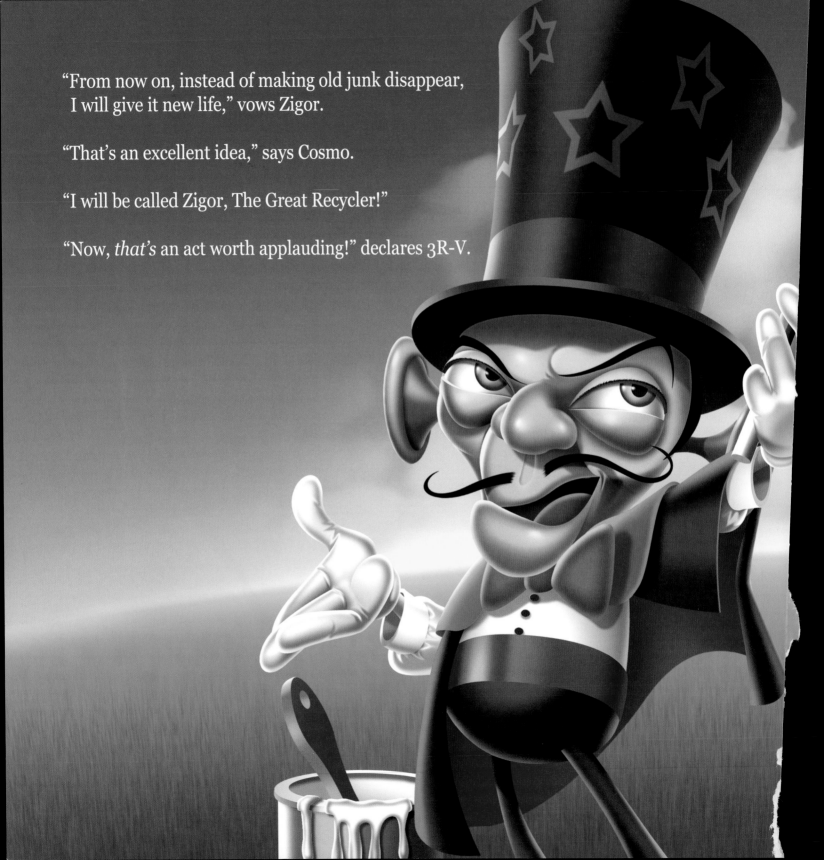

"From now on, instead of making old junk disappear, I will give it new life," vows Zigor.

"That's an excellent idea," says Cosmo.

"I will be called Zigor, The Great Recycler!"

"Now, *that's* an act worth applauding!" declares 3R-V.

After they say fond good-byes to Zigor, Cosmo and 3R-V take off for new adventures.

"Zigor is going to have great success with his new act," says Cosmo.

"I think you're right," says 3R-V.

"At least we know his first act with you was sensational.
Now, let's go find some dodos!" shouts Cosmo.

3R-V is a kind and gentle robot-ship invented by a scientist
on the planet Earth. This scientist cared a great deal about nature
and the environment. He built the robot-ship according to the following
principles: reduce, re-use, and recycle. He named the ship 3R-V and gave
it a propulsion system that uses a renewable, non-polluting source of energy.
3R-V is also equipped with incredible technological resources.

3R-V is Cosmo's best friend, and, together, they travel from planet to planet
in search of other dodos.